Dear Parent:
Your child's love of reading starts here!

I Can Read Books have introduced children to the joy of reading since 1957. Featuring award-winning authors and illustrators and a fabulous cast of beloved characters, I Can Read Books set the standard for beginning readers. From books your child reads with you to the first books they read alone, there are I Can Read Books for every stage of reading:

SHARED READING
Basic language, word repetition, and whimsical illustrations, ideal for sharing with your emergent reader

BEGINNING READING
Short sentences, familiar words, and simple concepts for children eager to read on their own

READING WITH HELP
Engaging stories, longer sentences, and language play for developing readers

READING ALONE
Complex plots, challenging vocabulary, and high-interest topics for the independent reader

ADVANCED READING
Short paragraphs, chapters, and exciting themes for the perfect bridge to chapter books

Every child learns in a different way and at their own speed. Some read through each level in order. Others go back and forth between levels and read favorite books again and again. You can help your young reader improve and become more confident by encouraging their own interests and abilities.

A lifetime of discovery begins with the magical words, "I Can Read!"

HarperCollins®, ■®, and I Can Read Book®
are trademarks of HarperCollins Publishers Inc.

The Berenstain Bears and the Wishing Star
Copyright © 2005 by Berenstain Bears, Inc.

Printed in the U.S.A.
For information address HarperCollins Children's Books,
a division of HarperCollins Publishers,
1350 Avenue of the Americas, New York, NY 10019.

Library of Congress Cataloging-in-Publication Data
Berenstain, Stan.
    The Berenstain Bears and the wishing star / by Stan and Jan Berenstain.—1st ed.
      p.   cm. — (An I can read book)
    Summary: Sister Bear learns about the magic of the wishing star, but Brother Bear teaches her that
hard work is also important.
    ISBN 0-06-058347-9 (pbk.) — ISBN 0-06-058346-0
    [1. Wishes—Fiction. 2. Bears—Fiction.] I. Berenstain, Jan. II. Title. III. Series: I can read book.
PZ7.B4483Beli 2005   2004022102
[E]—dc22   CIP
                                                                                 AC

www.harperchildrens.com
Typography by Scott Richards

1 2 3 4 5 6 7 8 9 10

First Edition

An I Can Read Book™

The Berenstain Bears and the WISHING STAR

Stan & Jan Berenstain

HarperCollins*Publishers*

One day the Bear family went to the mall.

They passed the toy store.

They looked in the toy store window.

"What a beautiful teddy bear!" said Sister.

"It's okay," said Brother.

"If you like teddies."

"Well, I do," said Sister,

"and I *love* that teddy."

Hmm, thought Papa,

Sister's birthday is coming.

Mama had the same thought.

That night the cubs were doing their homework.

Brother was making a map of Bear Country.

Sister was doing numbers homework.

She was not doing well with numbers.

She got a C on her last report card.

Papa was helping her.

She wanted to get a B or even an A.

Soon it was bedtime.

"Look!" said Mama.

"The wishing star."

"What is the wishing star?"
asked Sister.

"It is the first star that comes
out at night," said Mama.

"You can wish upon it."

Then Mama said the wishing star rhyme:

"Star light, star bright,

first star I see tonight.

I wish I may, I wish I might

have the wish I wish tonight."

"What happens then?" asked Sister.

"If you wish hard," said Mama,

"and you do not tell anyone your wish,

it *might* come true."

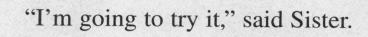

"I'm going to try it," said Sister.

She said the rhyme:

"Star light, star bright,

first star I see tonight.

I wish I may, I wish I might

have the wish I wish tonight."

Then Sister fell asleep.

She dreamed of the beautiful teddy.

Sister's birthday came.

She got the teddy for her birthday.

"I got my wish! I got my wish!" she cried.

After supper and birthday cake,

Sister and Brother did their homework.

Brother was still working on his map.

Sister was still working on numbers.

Getting a B or even an A would be so nice,

she thought.

That night Sister made another wish.

She said the wishing rhyme again.

Then she fell asleep and dreamed.

She dreamed about getting a B or even an A.

Sister got her report card the next day.

She got an A for numbers.

"I got my wish! I got my wish!" she cried.

Brother got a good report card, too.

They got a reward.

They were allowed to stay up

and watch a special TV show.

It was about a pony—

a beautiful, white pony.

Sister fell in love with that pony.

That night she said the wishing rhyme again:

"Star light, star bright,

first star I see tonight.

I wish I may, I wish I might

have the wish I wish tonight."

Then she went to sleep and dreamed.

She dreamed about the beautiful pony.

REPORT CARD
Sister Bear

NUMBERS	A
LANGUAGE	B+
SPELLING	A

The next morning
she woke up early.
She ran downstairs.

She ran outside to look for her new pony.

She looked all over.

It wasn't tied to the fence.

It wasn't in the shed.

It wasn't anywhere.

Sister was very sad when she came back.

"What's the matter?" asked Brother.

"I did not get my wish," said Sister.

"What did you wish for?" asked Brother.

"I'm not supposed to tell," said Sister.

"You can tell if you don't
get your wish," said Brother.

"I wished for a beautiful, white pony,"
Sister said.

"Oh," said Brother. "You know, Sis,
you have to be careful with the wishing star.
If you are greedy or ask for too much,
the wishing star may not hear you."

"I got my first wish," said Sister.

"It was your birthday," Brother said.

"I got my second wish," said Sister.

"You worked hard for that A," said Brother,

"but a pony? I don't know about that, Sis."

Sister thought about that.

Then she smiled and said,

"Well, anyway, two out of three isn't bad."